Ink Sling

Flairs and Glairs
Publication House

"Ink Sling"

ISBN No: 978-93-90416-06-6"
1st Edition
Language – English and Hindi

Flairs and Glairs
Publication House
Regd. Under MSME Act.

Disclaimer

This is a work of fiction and solely represent the thoughts of the corresponding authors of the articles. Our editors have tried their best to edit the content of all the authors and check the plagiarism.

All the write-ups in this book are unique and are only published in this book.

In case any plagiarism or error is found, only the author is responsible alone, and not the publisher or the Compilers.

Cover Designing and Book Formatting
Shubham Shah

Acknowledgement

My primary thanks to God. I am blessed with the energy to be able to complete this anthology.
I am also thankful towards our whole team of "Flairs and Glairs Publication".
I am thankful to my parent's, Mr. Ashok Shah and Mrs. Archana Shah for trusting and supporting me always. And my friends and extended family to support in every step of life. And to provide me a surrounding where I can raise my voice for all types of issues.

Thank you, all the co-authors, without your support we would never be able to complete this anthology
.

Co Authors

1. Shubham Shah (Founder Flairs and Glairs)
2. Ishani Agarwal (Co Founder Flairs and Glairs)
3. Muskan Shah (Compiler)
4. Ganpat Gehlot
5. Amritanshu Kumar
6. Priyanka Bose
7. Shikhar Pathak
8. R. Susanna Celsia
9. Jeevitha. S
10. Kodambakam Venkata Sai Pratyusha
11. Shreya Gupta
12. Yamini Sona Vaishnavi
13. Priyadarshni Bose
14. Anumula Pravali
15. Hansika SR
16. Meghana Dumpala
17. Asraya Raj
18. Madhu Singh
19. Abhilash Sharma
20. Megha V
21. Sahina Ghugha
22. Christy Gnana Deepa. J
23. Sonal Tripathi Mishra
24. Chavi
25. Abhiram B
26. Rashi Sunder
27. Parul Sunder
28. Pinki Bansal

29. Samikhya Swain (Ikhya)
30. Harshvardini. M
31. Remya R. Pillai
32. Sakshi Jain
33. Ishani D P
34. Nivedhitha Patwari
35. Muskan Gupta
36. M.Shanmuga Priya
37. Pratham Mittal
38. Anushree Srivastava
39. Nithya Kanagaraj
40. Chahat Kanchan
41. Adarsh Kumar Priyadashi
42. Subhananthini. R
43. Kavitha p
44. Deepak Pradhan
45. Shruthi Abhinaya
46. Shijin Ravi C
47. Swosti Samarpita Sahoo
48. Jyoti Matania
49. Aishwarya
50. Khushi Rathore
51. Prashamsh.C.Kulkarni
52. Shivani Sarwade
53. Zainab Iqtedar
54. Shubham Shinde
55. Rahul Sain
56. Subhendu Kumar Dash
57. Deepjyoti Chowdhury
58. Madhu Kumari
59. Nanci Kabra

60. Prachi Shah
61. Resni Ramakrishnan
62. Dipti S.
63. Sheela Suman
64. Shaikh Abdul Wasee
65. Somya Mohanty
66. Sakshi Barad
67. Srishti Srivastava
68. G.S. Jameel Akhtar Yalagar
69. Heymonth Ninja
70. Aishwarya VJ
71. J. Josephine Jesika
72. Arya Ojha
73. Prachi Sharma
74. Gudiya Tiwari
75. Priya Sharma
76. Ashutosh Kumar
77. Indu Sharma
78. Amit Kumar Singh
79. Mekhala Ananth
80. Pallavi Prasad
81. Yogi Trivedi
82. Priyanka Varma
83. Minal Manjariya
84. Purva Upadhyay
85. Pragyan Panda
86. S. Sai Kartheek
87. Sonu Pradhan
88. Neeti Gupta
89. Sanjay Naik
90. Abhilash Rout

91. Akanksha Sinha
92. Reena Yadav
93. Bhavya Mishra
94. Pratyusha Pattanaik
95. Ujjwal Shree
96. Krishna Motwani
97. Abhigna Modigonda
98. Deepesh Pathak
99. Ipsita Panigrahi
100. Kushi Kothale
101. Nobil Initha J.
102. Sameeksha Pimple
103. Meghna Chatterjee

Shubham Shah

(Founder- Flairs and Glairs)

Shubham Shah, entrepreneur at "Flairs & Glairs" a brand with dynamics in events organizing and cultural educational pan INDIA, He is a 26yr. old guy who recently has entered, the digital platform of imprinting emotions. He has initiated with his own open mic platform to help budding poets and aspiring writers under his brand named as "Teekhe Zasbaaat"
He is a commerce graduate from Bhagalpur City of Bihar.
He says Writing has impersonated him since childhood and he has now been writing for over a decade!
Cooking, on the other hand, is his passion! He also mentions, trying out new things just tickles him!
When asked sir, Why SPICY EMOTIONS?

He smiled and added, "agar jasbaat teekhe na ho toh wo jasbaat kaha" Spices are all that blends! So do his words!
As a chef, he presents to you his dish! Hot and freshly served! Taste it! Feel it! Enjoy it! You can also find his writing in the Solo book "Teekhe Zasbaat" and 70+ anthologies. With his passion to explore opportunities across Platforms he is working with keen devotion and We wish him all the very best for his future ventures
Share your reviews on his

INSTAGRAM

@spicy_emotions
@shubham4shah

Or via email on

shubham2shah@gmail.com

To stay tuned to his work and opportunities follow his business Handles

INSTAGRAM   FACEBOOK   YOUTUBE

@flairsandglairs
@teekhezasbaaat

WEBSITE:

https://flairsandglairs.in/
https://flairsandglairs.com/

Ishani Agarwal

(Co Founder- Flairs and Glairs)

Ishani Agarwal
Born and brought up in Kolkata, she has done her schooling and college from here itself. She is doing her post-graduation at the moment. Ishani loves talking to people around, and is excited for this new beginning of hers! Been a Compiler for 35+ Anthologies, and in the process for more, also, co-authored in 100+ Anthologies, Ishani is very Happy with how her life is turning out now!
Insta handle: Ishani_agarwal_quotes

COMPILER
Muskan Shah

'I follow dreams to make them reality'
Muskan Shah, an Indian first, a girl from Jharsuguda, Odisha. Currently a Company Secretary Professional Student, followed her dreams of an Interior Designer.
A writer and a Poetess.
Being a writer, she writes all genre: stories, articles, quotes, content's, etc. And being a poetess, she writes poetries and Poems arc her forte. She has a dream to be known as a Poet in the world for her poetries and beautiful pieces.
She not dreams of being a writer but also working hard to fulfill the same. Her journey till date has been amazing by being a compiler of 7 Anthologies and a co-author of 50+ Anthologies.
Instagram Handle -The_Unpublished.Ink

My Writing Journey

Quite a story
like a morning glory
It became an addiction
To write different fiction
Always portrayed character's
as if some actors
To write little pain
And love stories in rain
I always danced somewhere
Finding a clue in parts of spare
It was happiness
To Write with something clueless
I enjoyed it the most
Wandering in stories of ghost
Making reel to reality
Filling pages that goes for eternity
To make people smile
With some stories cute & some fragile
I will try to write more and more
Which I hope people will adore.

<u>Co-Authors</u>

Ganpat Gehlot

<u>मुश्किलें जरुर है, मगर ठहरा नही हूं मैं</u>

मंज़िल से जरा कह दो, अभी पहुंचा नही हूं मैं
कदमो को बांध न पाएंगी, मुसीबत कि जंजीरें,
रास्तों से जरा कह दो, अभी भटका नही हूं मैं
सब्र का बांध टूटेगा, तो फ़ना कर के रख दूंगा,
दुश्मन से जरा कह दो, अभी गरजा नही हूं मैं
दिल में छुपा के रखी है, लड़कपन कि चाहतें,
मोहब्बत से जरा कह दो, अभी बदला नही हूं मैं
साथ चलता है, दुआओ का काफिला
किस्मत से जरा कह दो, अभी तनहा नही हूं मैं....

Amritanshu Kumar
ऑफिस वाला प्यार

मिले जब हम अनजाने से थे
मगर फिर भी कुछ कुछ पहचाने से थे
जो कभी दूर चलती थी नज़रें चुराकर
वो लड़की मेरे साथ आने लगी है
फिर से तुम्हारी याद सताने लगी है

दूर थी लेकिन फिर भी पास थी मेरे
हाँ,ऑफिस में वो लड़की साथ थी मेरे
बातें सुरु हुई,बातें बढ़ने लगी
चैन से सोने वाली रातें अब जगने लगी
रातें जगने लगी,बातें बढ़ने लगी
प्यार की एक कहानी अब गढ़ने लगी

जो लाती थी घर से अकेले का खाना
वो लड़की मेरे साथ अब खाने लगी है
जो रहती थी अक्सर दूर दूर मुझसे
वो लड़की अब पास मेरे आने लगी है
फिर से तुम्हारी याद सताने लगी है....!

Priyanka Bose
तुम्हें देखा नहीं कब से

तुम हे देखा नहीं कब से......
मुझे अपने हर दर्द का हमदर्द बना लो,
दिल में नहीं तो ख्यालों में बैठा लो,
सपनों में नहीं तो आँखों में सजा लो,
अपना एक सच्चा अहसास बना लो ।।

मुझे कुछ इस तरह से अपना लो,
कि अपने दिल की धड़कन बना लो,
मुझे छुपा लो सारी दुनिया से ऐसे
कि अपना एक गहरा राज बना लो।।
करो मुझे मोहब्बत इतनी कि,
अपनी हर एक चाहत का अंजाम बना लो,
ढक लो मुझे अपनी वाहों में इस तरह,
कि मुझे अपना संसार बना लो।।

आप फूल बन जाओ मुझे भंवरा बना लो,
आप चाँद बन जाओ मुझे चांदनी बना लो,
रख दो अपना हाथ मेरे हाथों में इस तरह,
कि मुझे अपने जीवन का हमसफर बना लो ।।

Sikhar Pathak
Definition of Love

Well, there is no definition of love,
But if the thought of losing her never blinked your sleep,
If you never felt unavoidable desires to hear her voice,

If you never experienced sulk to see her glimpse,
If her sadness had not became the moisture of your eyes,
If her un-pleasent never gave you self-anger,
If being near her never increased your heartbeat,
If life didn't seem beautiful to you with her smile,
If your sleep never came without her permission,
And if she never kissed on your forehead in the morning
dreams,

THEN, you never experienced love.......
AND even if you did, it was much below the bar which is
been set in the past by lovers like me ....

R. Susanna Celsia
The beauty of pain

The thorns i see ,are not favourable .
They are dark and ugly ,pain causing .
They tear my flesh and hurt me ,pain is all i have from thorns
.

If only i got rid of this thorn in my flesh ,
This same ugly thorn is not beautiful but ,protects my beauty
.

Leaves me sacrs of love but protects me from hatefull hands .
I always wanted to get rid of this thorn in my flesh ,but my
heart is thankfull that this wish never came true
Pain is beautiful!!!!

Jeevitha. S
<u>Stupendous Night View</u>

Her mind was filled with lots of chaos,
She lost her hope on things and felt low .
When she looked up at the sky ,
She was awestruck by the view !
When she observed the scenario of around her,
She understood the betterment behind things.
She realised that happiness depends upon how we conceive things.
She saw the enchantress even un that gloomy sky ,
Even the unilluminated nights shows exquisite in its own way ,
Stars glinting as diamonds in the dimness ,
The crystalline aerosphere expliciting peace ,
That stupefying glance made all her torments evanesce ,
There exists the glide of positive vibes .
She summoned more wisdom and insight ,
All her dejections flew away ;
And her eyes once again shimmered with jubilance .

Kodambakam Venkata Sai Pratyuksha
I Still Remember............!

The sounds of waves,
the tides that hug,
the collection of shells,
the ice-cream bells,
the prints of footsteps,
the sand built house,
I still remember,
the fragrance of beach!

Shreya Gupta
<u>एक नई पहल</u>

दो भारत को देखा है हमने,

एक भारत मे खाने की तड़प है,

तो दूसरे मे अनचाही ख्वाइशें पूरी करने की तरस है,

एक भारत मे टुकड़ा-टुकड़ा जोर कर सब घर बनाते,

दूसरे भारत मे घरो को तरह-तरह की कलाकृतियों से सजाते,

एक भारत मे देश के लिए दिन-रात जीते,

दूसरे मे सिर्फ स्वतंत्रता दिवस और गणतन्त्र दिवस मे याद करते,

कितना फर्क है न दो भारत मे,

एक छोटी-छोटी गलियों से बनता,

तो एक भारत महलो से सजता,

एक भारत मे तो सब सुकून से सोते,

पर दूसरे भारत मे अगले दिन की चिन्ता लेकर पल-पल मरते,

क्यों धन का इतना बटवारा है,

धन ने ही तो इन्सानियत को मारा है,

क्या यु ही बटा रहेगा देश हमारा?

या मिटा कर लकीरो को एक दिन बनेगा 'हिन्दुस्तान' हमारा।।

Yamini Sona Vaishnavi
<u>I am your constant ...</u>

Years back I met you to be a person ...
And today I look up at you as my life ...
I know you are not with me for the moment ...
But as time travels , it will connect you and me ...
My heartfelt thanks to you for giving me loads of memories
to relive ...
I think about those days where you held my hands ...
But now , to I find my palms empty hurts !
I think about those days when your eyes met mine...
But now , to find plain walls in front of me hurts !
I think about those days where you made me smile with your
promises ...
But now , my smiles are transforming into tears and my
hurting heart is bleeding !
Many a times I wonder why am I not able to deviate my
mind from your image...
Ultimately super power answered it telling that it is true love
that is ruling my heart !
I never knew when will I see you again . But ....
All I wanted to tell you was just one thing ; I am constant in
your nectar poisonous thoughts . Your constant ...Forever and
ever !

Priyadarshni Bose
<u>क्यू इतने जल्दि हम बड़े हो रहे है??</u>

म्मी की पल्लू, पापा के बहाएँ,
सबके लिए प्यारे सच्चे बच्चे,
मानो जैसे मासूमियत पर सब थे जान छिड़कते ।
वह लाल-पिली बर्फ की गोलाई तो मिट्टी-मिट्टी एक रुपया वाली
कुल्फी मलाई,
कभी गिल्ली डंडा तो कभी भागम भगाई कभी तो कमंबल मे कर
देते थे कुटाई,
ननी की सुरीली लोरी फिर भी न सोए तो सुनाती थी राजा-रानियों
की स्टोरी।
न पैसे के थे टेंसन,न थे लाईफ के डंडे
न थी कल की फिक़ न थी फ्यूचर के सपने।
लेकिन अब हो रही है कल की चिंता
और अधूरे लग रहे है अपने सपने।
सोचो तो उड़ जाती है रातों की निंदे।
पिछे मूड़ कर के देखों तो सब अपने दूशमन लग रहे है।
मंजिल की चाहत मे हम कहाँ खो से गए है,
क्यू इतने जल्दि हम बड़े हो रहे है??

Anumula Pravali
<u>A sad reality</u>

You feel dejected for locking down at home
They feel contented for saving lives at someones home.
You have been selfish for your own lives,
They have always been selfless for our lives
You started protesting,
They continued protecting
You begun offending…
They still pursued defending.
Don't raise your voice,
Because they are the only choice.
Grab a momemt for their appreciation,
Which reminds us of their dedication.
Doctors… the only rescuers!!
..the only champions!!

Hansika SR
Is waiting very hard?!

You feel like meeting them right now
And wish for their side for that forever.
Later pondering the possie with a" how?"
And realize we can't ping whatsoever!

Many secret prayers for them,
Knowing that they won't think about you,
Many jealousies upon people close next to them,
Waiting harder every day for in the end "I have you"!

A lot of what - ifs do pop up in mind.
A lot of fears haunt, turning you blind!
You remember them for your every cough
And realize they are never beside to sit and laugh

Waiting is not that hard,
Staying away by miles,
Concealing emotions behind fake smiles,
Yes, waiting is not that hard! Is it?

Meghana Dumpala
<u>Shrunken soul</u>

Burying my own heart
in the fields of your flesh
hoping you would
shower me with love,
and make me
blossom into an angel...
but your filthy actions
made me suffocate to death
and made my heart
crumble like a dry leaf,
which made me
shrink into a devil
which I never thought
I would be....

Asraya Raj
<u>Weeping smile</u>

Desparating fate make us apart,
Striking words hurt me a lot,
Still my love act as a corden.
However I never want negations,
Only my whispering sound I can hear.
Where the stars were silent,
For them account was well known.
And just same as what they have,
Whistling cry was in vain.
Nobody heard my pain of lossing soul,
I myself soothe the heart reluctantly.
Forget to live for me, for the life of
lovelorn.
Fully employed in seeing his life lively
with others,
Partially burned away.
Oh god I cant attain, fed up with dying
life.
Take me away please...Ahhh ohhh
weeping smile......

Madhu Singh

स्याही का टुकड़ा ।
मेरे हाथ से यूं होगया उखड़ा।
जब अपने साथ छोड़ देते है तो दर्द होता है पर जब कलम साथ
छोड़ दे तो मरने को जी करता है ।
कलम पर संसार टीका ,बिन इसके हर इंसान लाचार पड़ा ।

Abhilash Sharma

मेरी पहचान ,
एक पिता की लाड़ली ,
एक पति की घरवाली ,
एक माँ का मान ,
दोस्तों की बस्ती जिसमें जान
भाई की लड़ने की साथी ,
एक दादी की वो नाती ।।

Megha V
<u>The Sayings for The Man There</u>

You, The Man over there!
The world must understand
Men aren't meant to give commend,
You have a lot more feeling
Where your heart is hiding,
Just throw away them
Then you will be a gem.

You again, The Man over there!
Stop living for the society
and giving your brain anxiety,
You are a common creature
Who is blessed with good nature,
So you can show your emotions
And come out of your commotions.

"Live the life you want to live until you live."

Sahina Ghugha

तूफ़ानों से ने निकल गई है कश्ती,
मंज़िल पर पहोचना अभी बाकी है।
विवश हूं परिस्थिति के आगे,
ललकारना इनको अभी बाकी है।

न पूछिए ये परिस्थिति मुझे कैसे रंग दिखलाई है।
गैरो ने सहारा दिया, अपनों से ठोकर खाई है।
समय तुम्हारा था, अब हमारा होगा,
समय में बदलाव लाना अभी बाकी है।
विवश हूं परिस्थिति के आगे,
ललकारना इनको अभी बाकी है।

अनुभव मेरी उम्र नहीं, परिस्थिति मुझे दिलाई है।
पाठशाला से बेहतर, जीवन का ज्ञान सिखाई है।
अंधेरे में बिखरी है सुबह मेरी,
उसे समेट लाना अभी बाकी है।
विवश हूं परिस्थिति के आगे,
ललकारना इनको अभी बाकी है।

Christy Gnana Deepa. J
<u>Journey to the end of the world</u>

In the luminous bright image of dawn,
My journey starts off,
Excited and amazed,
to reach the journey dazzled.

Thrilled to take up trekking,
And it is mind-boggling,
The journey of adventure and happiness,
With great will and blessedness.

Journey to speak with nature,
Makes my heart pure and cool,
Dark shades and high cliffs,
Tremendous and peachy fabulous.

Sonal tripathi
<u>रहगुज़र</u>

वक़्त अपनी रफ्तार से गुज़र जाता है
मगर बहुत कुछ है जो वहीं ठहर जाता है|
रुकने वालों के लिए , कौन ही रुकता है दोस्त
गर्द पीछे और कारवां आगे निकल जाता है|

उसकी राहों में बैठ के हमने, बरसों उसका ही इंतज़ार किया
और वो बिना देखे ही आगे को बढ़ा जाता है|
सोचती हूँ कि उसके नखरे ना उठाऊंगी इस बार तो मैं
तब भी ये पाजी दिल हर बार पिघल जाता है|

वो कहता है अब कोई राब्ता नहीं तेरा मेरा
फिर भी वो जाते हुए मुड़ मुड़ के तकता जाता है|
अब मैं उसे याद हूँ भी या नहीं....मुझे मालूम नहीं
फिर भी उसके हर किस्से में, मेरा ज़िक्र आ ही जाता है|

लोग कहते हैं, कि वक़्त के साथ सब कुछ ही भूल जाता है
पर कभी कभी कोई हम सा भी मिल ही जाता ह

Chavi

<u>Big brother and small brother</u>

Comparing both of them in difficult for me. But they both are
best.
Big brother always tease me and small brother never do
sharing with me.
One talks online with me but one is always talks offline with
me.
But both are equal for me. They both treat me equally.
Big brother calls be angry bird. But small brother always
confuse in speaking my name
Name of both brothers starts with letter R. It's very funny for
me
I am very lucky to have my both brothers #big and small
brother.
Love you both of my brother.

Abhiram B.

War doesn't bring peace,
If it has to do with peace.
Rather, it forces everyone
To bring into the war,
Causing devastation of everything
And nothing else.

If peace has to be brought back,
First love the culture, diversity
And uniqueness of a society,
Then you can advise them
In a polite manner
Which all are right and wrong.

Rashi Sunder
<u>किताब</u>

यह किताब कितना कुछ सह लेती है,
किसी का दुख, किसी का दर्द, किसी का प्यार संजो लेती है।
सदियों का इतिहास अपने में दफन कर लेती है,
आने वाले समय की सब बातें अपने में लिख लेती है।
कौन अपना, कौन पराया इसका हिसाब ले लेती है,
यह ज्ञान और विज्ञान की जानकारी भी हमें बयां कर देती है।
यह प्यार, दर्द, सुख-दुख सब समेट लेती है,
हमारे सपनों को अपने पर लिख लेती है।
इसमें इतना खजाना छुपा है,
पर इसे कोई चोरी नहीं कर सकता।
समझो तो ज्ञान का खजाना, ना समझो तो मामूली किताब,
जो पड़े वो पंडित, को ना पड़े वो अज्ञानी,
एक किताब कितना कुछ सह लेती है,
किसी का दुख किसी का दर्द किसी का प्यार संजो लेती है ।

Parul Sunder

<u>सबूत</u>

ये दुनिया हर काम का सबूत मांगती है,
तुम क्या हो उससे किसी को कुछ नहीं लेना देना,
तुम क्या हो वो बाद में जानेंगे,
पहले तुम्हारे हुलिए से तुम को पहचानेंगे,
जुबान पे अंग्रेजी कपड़ों पर ब्रांडेड टैग,
जुल्फे है सुनहरी मिज़ाज में नखरे,
यही है आज की इंसान की पहचान।
क्योंकि दुनिया में ईमान की बात नहीं होती,
ये दुनिया तुम्हें बाहर से पहचानती है,
अंदर से तुम क्या हो- यह बाद की बात है,
तुम्हारे अंदर क्या हुनर है- वह बाद में देखेंगे,
पहले तुम्हारे होलिए से तुम्हे पहचानेंगे।
पहले इंसान की पहचान,
बाहर से फिर जुबान से,
फिर अंदर से पहचानती है,
ये दुनिया हर बात का सबूत मांगती है।

Pinki Bansal
<u>मोहब्बत की सच्चाई</u>

दिल्लगी करते है लोग,
अपना दिल बहलाने को...
पहले वाकिफ़ होना
मोहब्बत से,
फिर बात करना किसी से
दिल लगाने को...
चार दिन की बेहया मोहब्बत
होती हैं जिस्मों सें,
ये मोहब्बत है लोगों की
मोहब्बत कहलाने को...
अगर गलतफहमी से मिले
महबूब किसी ओर की बाहों में,
तो ज़नाब बात करते हैं
उन्हें छोड़ जाने को...
उन्हें छोड़ जाने को...
ये मोहब्बत है लोगों की
मोहब्बत कहलाने को...

Samikhya Swain (Ikhya)
<u>You</u>

The lava is red
And my love for you,
Is still not dead.

The sky is blue,
I know,
It's colour matches with you.

Your lips are pink,
You know ?
And I drew them through my ink.

Your heart is black,
As you give me heart attack.

Your dreams are high,
I understand why !

Though my love is yellow,
And I say " I love you bloody Fellow "

Harshvarshini. M
<u>Invisibl</u>e

Initial happiness blasted my presence in the World
Later my happiness survived me to live long.
Drastic world commence to the change over
Nothing made us to come forward and
Nothing has changed in the existing world.
Time advances, something made me invisible to change in
human.
Featureless mind with thoughts and ideas,
Contrasting beauty of nature to be admired
That sometimes gives us nostalgic memories,
And thoughts of human to be changed.
Invisible to switch them from greedy thought in their heart.
Cover your heart with beauty and carry out with happiness.
Nothing made you to corrupt your own heart,
Its our own contemplation of mind disruption.
I get into human heart to purify themself.
Nothing in world is impossible to change similarly our heart
does....

Remya R Pillai
The detached love-story

Both of us are connected by the language of music;
the rhythm of which flows through our hearts.
Our ears echo the same song always,
let it be melody, pop, or jazz.

Yet when the music is played, we get separated,
our hearts yearn to be together.
In our soul, the music gets divided equally
but when we are let to be together,
it turns out to be a complicated relationship.

Again we get separated, play the same track
and again get complicated by entangling ourselves.
This isn't our unique story,
but is the story of every headphones,
who are the characters of a detached love story.

Sakshi Jain
<u>Secret Love</u>

Once upon a time, is Old and Fame .
I will give my story as a Secret Love Name.
Once a upon a time, there was a Little Charm ,
He was very Cute and had a Beauty that never Harm.
He used to Smile by looking on my Face's Smile.
And I also used to smile kissed.
Its all my Feeling towards Him.
Hey! you Prince Charm listen it's beat.
He was at a distance Mile that I thought I never Reached .
Its all my imagination,so God please make this True..
And I want my secret Love Story a wonderful True.

Ishani D P
<u>Dear Society,</u>

Why clothes are parameter for character?
Why gender dominates justice?
When kindness & sympathy are the root of Dharma,
then why you allow so much viciousness?
Why people have to suffer,
why you are still quite?
So much chaos is there, you have to make a change,
the right time has arrived.
Speak up, before the last bit of humanity is destroyed,
save your dignity, change your attitude.
It's time for you to change your outlook,
For the world to witness, a new revolution awaits.
Yours
Ever determined
Ishani_D_P_

Nivedhitha Patwari

Earth's maxmium hurdle will resolve if you
Permit your voice to be belived by yourself
And by accepting your drawbacks
To overcome the false impression you composed by yourself
and
To create constructive thoughts sharper and brighter by
Making negativity expensive.

Muskan Gupta
<u>Jo khud ki soche usey khudgarz...</u>

Jo khud ki sooche ussey khudgarzkehte hai...
Jo har baat par rang badale ussey girgit kehte hai...
Jo jhoothi khushi tum par jataaey ussey namakool kehte hai...
Jo sacchi baaton mein dhong kare ussey milawati kehte hai...
Jo khud chocholate manga Kar dusre se share kre... Ussey
bloody kamini kehte hai..
Aur...Jo bhagwaan krishna ke naam par logo ko bhul jaaey
ussey ladkiyon ka pyaar kehte hai ...

M. Shanmurga Priya
<u>Sky latern</u>

Dull and dark begins with a
memories of the past lurk in the way.
The little flicker of the flame.
It begins to grow,
In that soft brightness.
I have never felt so bright,
Our heart are now lighter than air.
It carries our hope and dreams.
A lot of sky want to see note,
I can not write everything.
I have to see- " We will stay as I wish",
Yes, you can say more in the small note,
When it shines our divine souls.
Fly high with purity and grace,
The flame never goes out,
Like the lights in the sky.
Be bright like sky Latern.

Pratham Mittal
Pure Imagination

Come with me and you will be
In a world of pure imagination
Take a glance and you will see
Into your imagination
We'll begin with a spin
Traveling within the world of my creation
What we'll see will defy Explanation
If you would like to look at paradise
Simply shop around and consider it
Anything you would like to, do it
Want to vary the planet, there's nothing thereto
There is no life I do know
To compare with pure imagination
Living there, you will be free
If you truly wish to be
There is no life I do know
To compare with pure imagination
Living there, you will be free
If you truly wish to be

Anushree Srivastava
Trust

If broken once, can never be earned again....
No matter how hard you try, it's all gone....
No matter how much you crave, it will never be all same
again....

pg. 39

No matter how many times you have had abandoned your
joys, it will all seem to be overshadowed by the lust.....
No matter how divine the connection was, it will always be
stained....
No matter how much you were a sacred soul to someone, you
will only be considered as a tainted being.....

No matter how much you loved and adored each other,
"We" will never happen in a lifetime......
//

Nithya Kanagaraj
<u>Hey Dad!</u>

You're that slender streak
Of morning sky,
The naive sun gleams - gently
Unfurls over the moon
Light lustred sky.
Aww! Guess what?
You wrapped me with warmth
At all my blues
And shared the frosty bites,
On all my torrids.
I am making a wish.
Will you take me to
Those stars, on your shoulders?
'Cause I wish,
I must be the first to land
On a star, carried by a Sun!

Chahat Kanchan
<u>कुछ अल्फ़ाज है ज्यादा एहसास है ...!!</u>

एक शख़्स में भी अकसर एक शख़्स होता है,,
और हम उस शख़्स से बेखबर होते है!!
बिलकुल वैसे जैसे ;, हम नही जान सकते किसी का दर्द जब तक
हम उसकी जगह पर नही होते है!!
प्यार ,, महोब्बत,, इश्क सब करते है ,, पछताते वो है जो किसी के
जाने के बाद भी किसी के नही होते है!!
बिलकुल वैसे जैसे कि आपकी कलम में अल्फ़ाज कम कुछ,,
एहसास कुछ ज्यादा होते है!!
कितना बुरा है सहना,, किसी शख़्स का यू दूर होना,, जो बेवफा भी
ना हो ,, फिर भी मजबूर हो जाए!!
एक को आगे बढ़ाना हो,, और एक यू दूसरे के लिए मगरूर हो
जाए!!
बिलकुल वैसे जैसे
रोना भी हो पर आंसू ना आए,,
हँसना भी हो ,, पर मुस्कुराना ना आए
और जिंदगी भी हो पर जीना ना आए!
ऐसे ही हर अधूरी दासताँ पूरी नही हो सकती ,,
जहाँ प्यार है वहाँ मजबूरी नही हो सकती ,,
मत लगाना दिल,,अपने दिल को बहलाने के लिए,,
महोब्बत किसी की जिंदगी से ज्यादा जरूरी नही हो सकती!!

Adarsh Kumar Priyadashi

Wrong decision

Throughout the years
She still holds you so dear
Restless heart with fears
That drought won't come after tears.
I know I was a wrong decision
But she still love you from bottom.

Within this rocky timeline You were her safe lifeline
Holding her up through the lows
Nurturing her through her growth
Though everything has a finish line
She refuses to approach this coming end.

Subananthini. R
<u>Her Aroma</u>

Her scents are all over me,
And all around me,
But I never get tired of it once
Still with the same radiance,
Like a new winter blossom,
She blooms everyday to make my life awesome
Her fragrance is unique
That makes me gald, though I'm sick
Hundreds of flower can't give me
The warmth, the feeling, and the happiness
From her delicate fragrance.
And I want to feel her aroma myself like a selfish elf.
Holding her hand and feeling her love
I wish to pursue what I'm now...

Kavitha P
<u>SHE IS SEARCHING</u>

She is searching
She is searching everywhere
In the pages of books
In the corners of house
In the world of people
In the stars of twilight sky
And in the rest of the universe

She is searching
She is searching for a piece
She is searching for a piece of peace!

pg. 45

Deepak Pradhan

आंखों में अनेक ख़्वाब सजाये,
दिल में लेकर बैठा हु!
दिल उसकी यादे सजाये,
धक् धक् करता उसके नाम से!
पथ प्रगति पथ पर चलने दे,
दीपक सदा तू जलने दे!
प्रगति पथ में लाख काटे हे मेरे,
उन काटो पर चलने दे!
खुद में तुझको धैर्य है रखना,
पथ पर तुझको अकेले बढ़ना हे!
न तू कभी थका हे
न तू कभी झुका हे
जीवन भर तू निरंतर चला हे,
अपने होसलो को रख दीगर में तू बड़ा हे!
जीवन की लीला है ये प्यारी,
यही तो तेरी सब से अच्छी यारी हे!
इसी में लगती दुनिया न्यारी,
ओर तेरी दोस्ती दुनिया से न्यारी हे!

Shruthi Abhinaya

You're there when I'm down,
You're there when I cheer up,
May be I don't notice much,
May be I don't pay attention,
But he always does.
Like a gift wrap,
You cover me.
You've never mind licking
My dull and sad dirty face.
Following me like a bug,
You've always been there with me...
Someone whom I'm never done with,
My four pawed friend.

Shijin Ravi C
<u>Rainbow</u>

The rain after so long,
Climb to reap my heart,
What a feel to have a tea,
With the rain wash the day.

With nothing to do and learn,
I whispered quiet along to lean,
What a day to dream and scream,
With nothing painted till the beam.

Then I saw unmixed colours of hope,
With souls that dance to floor,
What a scene in the evening steam,
Surely impressed the way nature is build.

Soon the dark approached the day,
Filled with hands of cold bay,
Making me run a light to see,
Yet another night with a scar abroad.

Swosti Samarpita Sahoo
My Sister: My Tantamount Twin

She is someone who walk along me,
She is the one who add
spice to my life with laughter
and mischief.
She stands by me through
hook or by crook,
Of course we cherish our
sisterhood.
She is the one who understands how I feel,
And there are times when
she see me crying,
Her heart would nearly bleed.
A special relationship is
what we enjoy,
It's a bond that is hard to
destroy.

Jyoti Matania
<u>She lends her pen to thoughts of emotions</u>

Here I am once again
Holding my pen while
it's going all dry

Though one writes about
Humanity, Equality, Neutrality, Justice and
such other terms routinely; however, it is a pen not character;
otherwise the entire world was at peace.

The pen mirrors
language and character:

But today it scares the hell out of me
With no stories there to write Nor remarkable date for me to
scratch...

The way my soul became so numb

That all my papers turn into blanks.....

Aishwarya
Dear ex- bestie

If a relation goes wrong, two people are equally responsible
for it.
I may have hurt you unintentionally, I realised and
apologized to you later.
This doesn't mean you were never wrong , you have hurt me
at times ,
But you didn't even bother to apologize .
There were times when I was struggling to smile,
But you didn't turn up for me.
I did everything for you like any friend who cared for you
would do,
I was happy doing that without expecting anything in return.
Then , the time for test of our friendship came.
One fine day , you heard something from somebody,
At the most important time to trust me , you simply didn't
This broke me completely.
I'm completely done with my one-sided efforts to save our
relation,
Realization dawned upon me of how friendship would never
go back to normal.
I know we both are happy now, but trust me I will always
keep you in my prayers.

Khushi Rathore
नजरअंदाज कर देगा क्या?

मैं मिलूँ अगर किसी मोड़ पर,
मुझे नजरअंदाज कर देगा क्या?

किताब-ए-जिन्दगी में,मसले को हमारे,
मुलाकात-ए-राज़ कर देगा क्या?

हाँ,मरीज हूँ तेरे ख्वाबों की,
हकीकत बनाकर,इनका इलाज कर देगा क्या?

यूं खामोशी से मुँह मोड़ कर,
इश्क को मेरे,नाराज कर देगा क्या?

आँसू छुपाकर खुद के, निगाहों को,
गमों की दराज कर देगा क्या?

मैं मिलूँ अगर किसी मोड़ पर,
मुझे नजरअंदाज कर देगा क्या?

Prashamsh.C.Kulkarni

I pray to sink,
Sink in the deep bottomless sea of love
I pray to see
See the darkest, silent, tranquil depth
It's excruciating and suffocating to be alone
So I pray, that someone sinks with me,
But I can only crave
Because all I see are running rivers and shallow ponds
Beautiful and rave
Set on a longing quest of the great sea,
Young and gullible to break bonds
So, I pray, to find the sea
And I pray to sink

Shivani Sarwade
<u>बेहिसाब</u>

माना की हम तुमसे
बेहिसाब लढते है।
मगर सच बताऊ तो,
तुम्हे खोने से बेशक डरते है।

अगर तुम होते हो साथ तो,
लबों पे मुस्कुराहट हम
लाजवाब रखते है।

मगर जाते हो तुम तो,
बेमिसाल उन लम्हों को याद
करते हुए हम रो जरुर पडते है।

Zainab Iqtedar

Tears aren't bitter
if they heal you from inside
as they seep into the cracks
of your fragile facade
perhaps they might glue
your splintered soul together
or perhaps they might render
you speechless with sorrow

and laughter isn't joyous
if you can't feel it inside
as it flows from your lungs
to the curves of your lips
perhaps it might soften
the sharp edges of your pain
or perhaps it might become the language
of your soul screaming in vain.

Shubham Shinde
<u>नज़रों से नज़रें....</u>

तैर कर पायाब-ए-दरियां पार कर जाऊँगा,
तेरे इश्क़ में कुछ इस तरह हार कर जाऊँगा,

सौदा-ए-जिस्म का हमनें कभी किया नहीं,
मगर इन लफ़्ज़ों से क़त्ल-ए-आम कर जाऊँगा,

नज़रों से नज़रें मिलाकर हर्ज जो भी हुई थी,
मिल्कियत में अपनी फ़िर तेरे नाम कर जाऊँगा,

भूल गया है वो जमाना उस वक़्त के मोहताज को,
मगर इस वक़्त में भी तुझे चाहकर मर जाऊँगा,

फ़िर किसी मयखाने में बैठ महफिलें सजाऊंगा,
दो घूँट तेरे नाम के फेंककर तुझे दिल से मिटा डालूंगा।

Rahul Sain

अंधेरा था शहर मे
मुझे बुलाया गया ,
मीठे लफ्जो से दिल बहलाया गया
जो झुकी नज़रे मेरी तमाशबीनों में
मेरे सामने मेरा घर जलाया गया

Subhendu Kumar Dash
<u>Self- expedition</u>

Neither from here nor from there,
I am not from then or now,
I am from the inception,
Busy in the quest of the end.
Let me solve my mystery,
Let me revisit my history,
So that I can find out my origin,
And try to end my being.
I am tired of my existence,
I am not interested in others,
I just want to return to the form,
Who brought me to this world.
I lost my own identity,
To find out my originality,
And now it's His turn,
To make me realize my nativity.

Deepjyoti Chowdhury
Finding a way out

If you're stuck with multiple doubt,
Know that there is always a way out.
If temptations try to knock you out,
Be an exception and proudly stand out.

Problems are a part of this life,
Be bold and gently move with a swipe.
Happiness and sorrow is a part of life,
You would face both agreement and strife.

The universe will help you to find a way out,
Keep your faith strong and never have a doubt.
When problem in your path is allowed,
Be patient and avoid being a lout.

There is always a solution to a problem,
Kill negativity and be filled with optimism.
Face all challenges with enthusiasm,
Set your goals and fix your vision.

Madhu Kumari
Education System

Education was our right.
Yes it was, about previous time.
In today's world,
Education is a business,
Fees are the gambling games.
Whatever will private universities demand,
You have to, serve them again and again.
They want money, we want degrees from them.
It's all about the exchange game.
Don't be shocked! keep calm,
We are just going back in the ancient days.
Those days of barter system,
Where you have to give one grain,
If you want other in exchange.
Nothing has changed.
Other people cannot be blamed.
Problem is in our brains.
We want to get in these gambling traps,
So that we can flaunt our degrees,
We are the products of the famous brands.

Nanci Kabra

कुछ कहना था मुझे तुमसे पर लफ्जों ने साथ नहीं दिया
मैंने गुजारिश की कई बार उनसे की मुझे कहने दो
पर उसने एक सवाल किया और मैं थम रह गई

जब उसे तुमसे फर्क नहीं पड़ता तो तुम्हारे लफ्जों से क्या फर्क पड़ेगा

जिसे जाना है वह तो कभी आया था ही नहीं

और जो आया है तुम्हारे पास, उसे तो जाना ही नहीं

तो मैंने पूछा उससे कि आया क्या था मेरे पास

तो उसने मेरी आंखों से आंसू बहा दिया

मेरी चढ़ती हुई इमारत को एक शन में गिरा दिया।।

कुछ कहना था मुझे तुमसे पर लफ्जों ने साथ नहीं दिया

तुम्हें जाते देख तुम्हें जाते देख ये खामोश हो गए

कि तुमने पूछा हमसे कि तुमने हमें रोका क्यों नहीं

यह बताओ जब तुम जा रहे थे मुझे कौन सा हक दिये जा रहे थे

तुम्हें रुकने का हक तो उसी समय रुक गया

तुम्हें रोकने का हक तो उसी समय रुक गया

जब तुमने कहा था मैं जा रहा हूं

इस बार खुद को नीचे गिराना, इसने मुझे यह एहसास नहीं दिया

बहुत कुछ दिया इसने तुम्हारे जाने के बाद

यह कलम यह कागज और इनका साथ दिया

Prachi Shah
To my lost best friend

I considered u as my soulmate,
But we turned into strangers,
My love for you was possessive,
But u taken that in a wrong way.

We had a good run in life,
Our memories are unforgettable,
Yeah I missed u a lot,
But now I don't want u anymore.

No one can deny I cried a lot,
I didn't found you anywhere,
when I needed u the most,
Friendship breaks heart too,
That scary day made me realize too.

I tried a lot to clear gap between us,
Something is not meant to be forever
Our broken friendship proves that too.

Resni Ramakrishna
Mystery in Greenwood

Cascade of pain flowing inside,
my mind messed up like maze.
Wrinkles hid my beauty, but
the flow inside is still young.
Preaching for a good time,
I always had a bad dream.
Blinking with frozen heart,
magic was the only hope.
I roaming between hazelwood,
with wilder heavy heart.
The more fruitful I am,
the more cunning they are.
My heart skipped a beat,
on seeing the mystery behind greens.
I found answers, from silent breeze.
Greens with pink blossom,
led my life to a magical start...

Dipti S.
Seasons

Seasons...
Seasons keep changing.
Be it winter, summer, spring and fall.
If you observe closely.
All of them seem to teach you something.
Winter teaches you to be icy cold when you need to be.
Summer shows you to be hot as a blazing fire.
Spring tells you to bud and blossom.
And, finally Autumn teaches you that it is okay to fall.
But, each and every time you fall, you should get back up
again.
And, that is how you grow.
It paves a way to your budding and blossoming!
These seasons show you that all of this moulds you, sculpts
you.
They also show you that change is the only constant.
They are wise enough to show you that this is life.

Sheela Suman
प्रेम

अहंकार गर है एक पत्थर
तो ज्ञान में होता है प्रवाह !

अहंकार में जड़ता है
पर प्रेम में होता है बहाव!

अब शीतल जल की धारा बनकर
जग को शीतलता , तुम दे दो!

जीवन मरण से ऊपर उठकर
नाम को अपने अमर कर लो!!

Shaikh Abdul Wasee

मैं हूँ तो मेरी सोच हैं,
मेरी सोच हैं तो मैं हूँ ।
मैं हूँ ही कितना सा,
इस बड़े जहां में एक कण सा।
दर्द मे भी खुलूस सा,
आज़ार मे बेकरार सा,
नफरत में भी उन्स सा।
मैं कौन हूँ ये सवाल हैं मुझे,
सवाल का जवाब भी सवाल लगे मुझे।
तुरबत को मुनतजीर हो गया मैं,
अपने ही ताबीर-ओ-तीरगी मे खो गया मैं,
कोई राह दिखाई न दे अब मुझे,
मुखतसर ही खुद में बचा हूँ मैं।
मैं क्या करूँ जो मुझे सुकून दे,
बेखुदी मे फना, या फकत जीने का तो जुनून दे।
मैं ही हकीम, मैं ही गुलाम हूँ,
बैठा हुआ फिर भी सफर पर हूँ, छूने चला मक़ाम हूँ।
तखय्युल टुटा और आँखें खुली तो जाना,
आफत-ए-ज़माँ में फसी, खुद की आवाम हूँ।

Somya Mohanty

<u>ख़ामोशी</u>

लफ़्ज़ों की "फ़क़ीर"
में " खामोशी " से मशहूर हूँ
मुर्दा समझे हमेसा ये दुनिया मुझे
पर में एहसासों का एक "ताबीर" हूँ (२)

ना पढ़ने की ज़हमत करे कोई दिल यहाँ

ना रंग कलम की लेख चढ़ि हैं

बेरंग की छबि कहे हर शक्स मुझे

में एक पुकार हूँ धड़कन का ,बस जज़्बात से मेरी रूह जुड़ी हैं (२)

तरह तरह के दर्द सजा इस ज़िन्दगी में

सात रंग की इश्क़ भी समाए

में एक आश्रा हूँ हर बेसहारा का

अबसोस हैं सिर्फ ,मुझे कोई ना समझे (२)

खुशि भरी दौलत जात की

भरे यहां आंगन सदा

दामन भी ना हो किस्मत में जिसकी

दुनिया उसके सामने बस ब्यापार जैसा (२)

हैं कटिपतंग के भी सपने

चाहे वो छोटा ही सही

तुम बून्द हो मेरे उस गहराई का, मुझे मानो तुम समन्दर कभी (२)

Sakshi Barad

<u>पंछी</u>

कभी कभी इन पंछीयोसे नफ्रतसी होती है,

इसलिए नही की इनकेपास पंख है

और मेरेपास नही....

बल्की इसलिए ..

की ये आसानीसे आसमान छू लेते है

और मै इतने कोशिशो के बाद फिर भी नही.....!!

<u>राह</u>
ऐ राह तू तो जानती थी ना...

इस मोडपे मेरी मंजिल नही..
फिर मुझे रोका क्यू नही ...!!

कमी
कभी खुदमे किसिको ढुँढा करती थी,
आज मुझे खुदमे मेरीही कमी महसूस हुई ...!!

Srishti Srivastava

तुझपे ही मेरी जान
तुझपे ही निसार
तू ही मेरा प्यार
मेरा हमदम मेरा यार

तू ही ख्वाब है मेरा
तू ही सच है
तेरे बिना है नहीं मेरा संसार
मेरे दिल का पल पल का विचार
मेरा हमदम मेरा यार

तेरे बिना मैं अधूरी
तुझको पाकर हो जाऊं पूरी
तुझसे कहना है बारम्बार
तू ही मेरा हमदम तू ही मेरा यार
ओ मेरा हमदम मेरा यार

G.S. Jameel Akhtar Yalagar
<u>Will Rise Again</u>

I have enjoyed the blossoms, have gone through the rashes.
Have seen the burning, gone through the churning.
Fire has burnt me that's not all I see.
I have failed this time, it's not gonna be same everytime.
Life has never been like a song,my heart knows suffering for
long.
Every time I wear a smile,To hide pain that's a style.
Everyone has hard time actually that's the time to shine.
Failure is not for cowards,It's for the hardest.
Success has very big demands,small are not the rewards.
This fire will burn next is my turn
I will fight the rashes,shall rise from the ashes.
I will rise again,I will bloom again
To bring that smile back again.

Heymonth Ninja
A random dot

It is a pen which lost its blood,
A drop of ink can cause flood:
Believe yourself before you write,
Rotate the sky by flying as a kite...

Sentences call me as a ugly dot,
Without me, they are meaningless a lot;
I can twist their work with fun---
Consider me as a bullet and them as gun!

It is I who draw the tiny world,
Of dark books that should to be sold;
Do you ever think, "You are a waste?",
Prove your need by creating new taste;

Join with other dots to form as a word,
Pierce the tongue of every devil lord!!
A random dot can strike out the paper,
The situation bless you to be a trapper.

Aishwarya VJ
The Spice of life

Along the kitchen cabinet I see,
the ingredients of tea.
Life is like a food I say,
Yes,said my bae.
Childhood went like a smoothie,
now I kind of feel croupy.
Teen started like a sweet donut,
even though it had so many 'do not'.
My anger is like a chilly,
I know it is very silly.
The next minute I will be cheesy,
posing for the photo 'Eee'.
So yeah,Life is a prize
it won't happen twice.

J. Josephine Jesika
A longing heart.

Thy eyes, is where I am lost,
All I want is thy love and thou art.
Longing for you to hold my hand,
To feel my warmth and to live on our own land.
You are not just my choice,
Yet, you are mineth inly rejoice.
Thy love makes me cure,
From the state of being obscure.
Thy presence is more than enough,
And I wish myself to be your better half.
Look deep down into my heart,
That beats your name telling that you are my sweetheart.
Now, I am not how I am meant to be,
Indeed, I am sunk in the thoughts of thee.

Arya Ojha
Power to empower

Oh, Girl you are a flower.
Shine with your smile,
Oh, Girl you can travel miles.
Not being an optional,
Oh, Girl you are phenomenal.
Twinkle with your work,
Oh, Girl you can achieve all perks.
Embrace your body,
Oh, Girl you are not anyone's copy.
Show your fighter spirit,
Oh, Girl you can have all merits.
Power to empower,
Oh, Girl you are a flower.

Prachi Sharma
<u>Can't help can't stop</u>

You are not helping me to fly.
Do you not help hand.
You are not improving me.
You don't put any effort on me.
You don't spend anything on me.

Why are you ready to stop me?
Why are you willing to break off my dream?
Is my dream nothing for you?
Without dream ,I am nothing.
Without dream , I just like
A bird without wings.
Without goals , I can't reach anywhere.

Have I no right to see dreams?
If I have right,then
Who gives you the right to stop me?
Why do all of you stand against me?
Can you not stand in my support?
If you can't help,

Gudiya Tiwari
Safar taali tak

Kismat ki bhi badkismati dekho,
Jo kismat khud samajh na payi hai;
Aayi takraane hm sarfiro se,
Aur khud muh ki usne khayi hai.

Apna sar par haath khuda ka,
Wahe guru ki parchayi hai;
Ishwar ne rehem bakshi hai,
God ne dua farmai hai.

Rah-e-manjil ke avi raahi hai hum,
Rah ke har archan se takra jayenge;
Hame girane ki koshish krne wale,
Apna astitwa gawa jayenge.

Bura nhi lgta kisi ki baato ka hame,
Kadr hai unke jasbaato ka hame
Warna, apne pe utar jaaye to dekhega jamana,
Gaali dene walo se bhi –
Taali hum thukwa jayenge.

Priya Sharma
Equilibrium

When action and reaction all goes same
when you don't really wonder about fame and shame
it took us ages to understand the fact it's not that complicated
, just a balancing act

when you follow truth for self enlightenment
and reached the point of divine contentment
when you niether show off imperium not afraid of facing
crematorium
thats when you get key to unlock your souls solarium
and that the moment when you inculate actual sense of
equilibrium

Ashutosh Kumar
बचपन के दिन

गुजर गया वो जमाना
जब हम भी नादान थे
दुनियादारी से कोई मायने न थे
हम वो थे, जिनके अरमान उड़ने के थे
बस, दादी-नानी से कहानियां सुनने के थे
दोस्तों के साथ बस ख्वाहिश खेलने के थे
हर चीज के लिए मां से जिद करने के थे
बारिश में कागज़ के नाव बनाने के थे
हर पलो को ख़ास बना लेने के थे
अपने-पराए के बीच फर्क न थे
स्कूल से आकर झूला ही अपना ठिकाना था
छुट्टियों में नानी गांव सबसे अच्छा आशियाना था
बचपन का वो जमाना था
जिसमें खुशियों का खजाना था
मौज-मस्ती से भरपूर वो जमाना था....

Indu Sharma
<u>सुनहरी यादें</u>

सुनहरी यादों को पिरोया है हमने
बना दी है अफ़सानो की माला

ऐसे कैसे भूल जाएँ
ये तो बताओ
तुम जो हो ना सके ग़र अपने
शायद वक्त को नहीं था गवारा
...पर ... इन वादों-यादों पर तो हक़ रहेगा हमारा

वसीयत में भी लिख जाएँगे
देख लेना
कुछ और का तो पता नहीं
... पर ...ये यादें किसी को ना देना

Amit Kumar Singh

एक एक लफ्ज जोड़कर उनका नाम लिखा
फिर उनके नाम अपना हर एक शाम लिखा
जब तन्हाई दबिश देने लगी बार बार
तो आने को करीब उनको एक पैगाम लिखा
रूठे यार को मनाने के लिए हालात-ऐ-बयान लिखा

Mekhala Ananth
How?

How do you light up this world so easily?
Are you family to the Sun that even NASA know nothing
about?
You are the one that scientists seek with a telescope, how did
you manage to navigate into my soul?
Travelling long and far, one goes to explore.
Travelling with you this far, I have been walking with my
home all along.
If life is a movie, I would have your scenes play in loop.
You rise with every breath and
I fall for you as you breathe.
Surely Earth loves us, with gravity it holds us, just as how
you embrace me.
Lost is all without you and
my love is always with you.

How do you do it?
Every string of my thoughts wind up to you.
How does your thread weave into my head? Sewing clothes
of warmth
And I just wear a smile, because Even Right Now
I am making way for you into my head.

Pallavi Prasad
छुपे जज़्बात

मेरे चेहरे में कितनी कलाकारी है,

pg. 81

पर यूँ मत समझना की मैं कलाकार हूँ ।
गम छुपाना कोई इस चेहरे से सीखे ,
पर यूँ मत समझना की मैं चोर हूँ ।
तेरी यादों में डूबी रहूं ,
पर कभी ये न सोचना की मैं पागल सी हूँ ।
तेरी गलतियों को मैं भूलती रहूं ,
पर कभी ये न सोचना की मैं नादान सी हूँ ।
तेरी हर मुश्किल को अपना बना लूँ ,
पर कभी यर न सोचना की मैं डरपोक सी हूँ ।
चलू मैं तेरे हर सफ़र में तेरे साथ ,
पर जो कभी न चल पायी ,
तो ये न सोचना की मैं थकी मुसाफ़िर सी हूँ ।।

Yogi Trivedi
एक हारा हुआ सच

ना समझ रहा है कोई और ना समझा जाएगा,
यह ऐसे हालात हैं जिसमे आदमी को परखा जाएगा।

चाहे वो शख्स हो बिल्कुल नादान,
मगर लोग तो लगाएंगे उसपे बेतूके इल्जाम।

आखिर क्यों? क्या हक है लोगों को किसी के बारे में बोलने का,
पहले खुद तो प्रमाण ले आए अपनी योग्यता का;
फिर मोल लगाएं अपने शब्दों से किसीको तोलने का।

अंदर से गुस्सा होते हुए भी बाहर से मुस्कुराना पड़ता है,
ऐसे ही हर बार एक सच को बेतूके झूठ के सामने हारना पड़ता है।

फिर भी है उम्मीद की पतझड़ में बरखा आएगी,
और फिर सच्चाई की मिसाल हर पल लहराएगी।

Priyanka Varma
And am the girl..!!

I'm the girl who hides behind a smile every day,
My pain and misery fall from the sky
So hard I try to ignore it, but it still gets by..
I'm the girl who has a tough exterior,
But that's not who I really am..
Surrounded with memories of what could have been,
The hatred screams under my skin..
I'm the girl who has a lot of problems
But doesn't share one thing..
I'm the girl who keeps everything bottled up..
Nobody knows the real me..
Nobody knows what I go through every day..
Nobody knows what I have to do just to make it through the
day..
Nobody knows that I'm the girl who isn't who I say I am..
And I'm the girl who cries herself to sleep every night just
trying to forget the pain..!!

Minal Manjariya
"क्या है जिंदगी?"

बस! एक छोटी सी मुस्कान के सहारे कट रहा सफर है जिंदगी,
ना जीने की चाह में जीने की उम्मीद सी हमसफ़र है जिंदगी।

कई बार आशाओं का तो कई बार निराशा का एक भंवर है जिंदगी,
ठहरी हुई ज़िन्दगी की किताब का उलझा हुआ 'कवर' है जिंदगी।

हरबार ना सही पर कई बार एक suffer है जिंदगी,
फिर भी!
बस! एक छोटी सी मुस्कान के सहारे कट रहा सफर है जिंदगी।

Purva upadhyay
Just talk to me

I know you are alone,
But it's your choice,
I wanted to talk with you,
But you don't want to,
Talk can heal your heart,
Heart that ache because of fate,
I know you are wise and clever,
But sometimes you need someone,
Someone who can understnd you,
It's your fate that happens to you,
But your fate can't decide your future,
Your future based on your decisions,
Make your desicions by yourself,
You are my sunshine and hope,
You are my inspiration,
You can't shattered like this,
You have to talk to me..

Pragyan Panda
Rourkela

The green city of Steel rather smart;
Yes the heart of Odisha.
A must visit to unique temples:
Hanuman vatika and hilltop for sample.

IG Park and dear park for amusement;
The Jubilee park for entertainment.
Well a peaceful place to stay,
A healthier place to portray.

With ample of markets of brands;
Cheaper ones with best trends.
They got the hub of street foods;
With local and foreign street goods.

Best is the fraternity of cosmopolitan:
That would make and recreate every battalion.
The city of life and happiness;
A tourist keeps craving for its essence.

S. Sai Kartheek
Ink slings

Cry of heart, smile of thought,
Sound of beat, feel of heat,
All the things and all the clings
Do form right into poems

Filled by mind's sensible columns
Just jumps on to the paper sheet
With all the force that they can meet
Harvest of a poet's pain
Cleaner than a diamond's shine
Holds up every kith an kin
As the soul of itself in a single line
From the atom to the phantom
Every here and there, shows it's glare
Makes the life a blissful share
Takes the life to greater fare
Heartfelt times lays foundation
Pen dealt writes makes manifestation
Tears of tears, laughs of laughs
Smiles of smiles, miles and miles
Writing all the way with pain and pleasure
Holding ink as a source of treasure
Equals nothing th…

Sonu Pradhan
A Letter to my Children -from your Mother

To my Children,

I love you my children
I care for you;
I shower my blessings on you
But what did you do?
You destroyed me!
Everyday pain caused by you is intolerable,
The greed that you have/had devasted me from within.
I am crying;
I am infuriated;
I am heartbroken;
I am sad;
I am angry for your ludicrous activities;
Dear Future generation;please save me and take a pledge that
you will too save your mother. From your Mother

Neeti Gupta
आत्मविश्वास

आत्मविश्वास जिंदा रखो हर हाल में
फिर सब नाचेंगे आपकी ताल पे
मन में जले आत्मविश्वास का दिया
अंधेरा भी कुछ ना बिगाड़ पाएगा
हौंसले से कांटे भी पुष्प बन जाते हैं
जो कतराते थे वे भी पास बुलाते हैं
आत्मविश्वास चरित्र रोशन कर देती है
तुच्छ इंसान की तो आत्मा भी मरती है
आत्मविश्वास बिना सराहता नहीं कोई
चलती जिंदगी तुम्हें ना बुलाता है कोई
आत्मविश्वास हो सब सलाम ठोकते हैं
आपके फिर सब तरफ चर्चे होते हैं
रखो आत्मविश्वास को मन में संजोकर
देखो दुनिया होगी बड़ी ही मनोरंजक
आत्मविश्वास का खजाना बड़ी
ही मेहनत से हासिल होता है
जो जमा कर ले इसे जिंदगी की
डोर में मोती रूपी खुशियां पिरोता है

Sanjay Naik
भाभी !!

कभी परिवार का सम्मान बन जाती है
तो कभी मां-बाप का अभिमान
रिश्तों को दृढ़ बनाने में लग जाती है
नहीं टूटने देती कभी अपना स्वाभिमान ।

कभी मां की तरह डांटने लग जाती है
तो कभी दोस्ती पर देती है थोड़ा ध्यान
कुछ सवालों के जवाब खुद बन जाती है
रीति-रिवाजों पर छलका जाती है अपनी जान ।

सादगी और विनम्रता से पेश आती है
तो कभी संस्कारो से चलाती है
घर के अरमान
सास-ससुर का दिल जीत लेती है
बड़ी मुश्किल से बनाती है अपनी पहचान।

Abhilash Rout
"Giggle" - Laugh Gently

Every human being in the world
try to enjoy some moments with
fun and enjoyment to live every
moments one needs to giggle.

The best way to express our
feelings are sometimes
that we can really go on a long
way as because we need to
understand the balance of life.

We should always remember
that laughing gently really
describe our nature in a
better and improved way.

Akanksha Sinha
<u>प्यार का एहसास</u>

प्यार एक एहसास है
जो खुद में ही ख़ास है
कभी खुशी तो कभी गम का आभास है
ज़िन्दगी की सबसे हसीं शुरुआत है
जो रूह से रूह में समां जाए
ऐसा इसका एहसास है
प्यार एक एहसास है
जो खुद में ही ख़ास है
जिसे मिल गया वो
जीत गया ये दुनिया
जिसे न मिला
उसकी लूट गयी दुनिया
हसीन सी है जिंदगी प्यार मे
मिल जाती है खुशिया प्यार में
दौलत का मोहताज़ नही ये
अपनेपन का एहसास है ये
प्यार एक एहसास है
जो खुद में ही खास है

Reena Yadav
<u>बाल मजदूरी</u>

हर बचपन खुशहाल नही होता,
घर पर रहने से पेट भर जाए यह हाल नही होता।

खेलने की उम्र से ही दुनिया सिखा दी जाती है,
किताब के बदले काम की सूची थमा दी जाती है।

क्यों वह हर बोझ उठा लेता है,
वह चार पैसे भी कमा लेता है।

पूछा जब मैने उस नादान से,
कह गया किताब उठाने की मन मे चाहता है।

मेहनत से ही तो अपनो को पालता हूँ,
हर बचपन खुशहाल नही होता आज यह भी मानता हूँ

Bhavya Mishra
Pen for pain

Someway or other
this anger lands up on me.
Generated from within,
is always a part of me.
Yet I blame others
their deeds, I see as sin.

I pray to almighty and him
both to trust me and bless,
control and hide from unworthy dream
Yet I suffer, more or less.

Oh! I am sad. Am I?
Will I be able to contain me?
Highly unlikely, yet I am full,
with agony, pain and hateful oceans?
O god bless the power to soul of my
For kindness to ungrateful.

Pratyusha pattanaik
Time

Tick tock...tick tock...
Life is counting down on your internal clock.
Memories that feel as if they occurred yesterday
turn to flashes of moments that seem to fade away.
People you once knew
walk by without a clue.
The times you once shared
exist as if you were never there.
Years fly...friends die...
and you never know when you'll say your last goodbye.
Oh, how I wish I could turn back time,
spend it with loved ones and cherish what once was mine.
Or to go back even more,
being a kid in a candy store.
How I miss the way I used to feel
on Christmas day when Santa was real.
But back to reality...back to today,
family is scarce and memories continue to fade away.
Tick tock...tick tock...
How I wish I could control this clock

Ujjwal shree
Rise and shine

It hurts...when people says that you have to change, But not their perception.
It hurts... When people says to my parents not to encourage to do what i want to, But not to their Taboo's.
It hurts... when people says that you won't fit in it, But not their customs and conventions.
It hurts....when people says that I m not normal because I want to try something new.
So what to do next...just skip it, Kick it and grow new normal...

Krishna Motwani
I don't cry,

I don't cry,
Because my parents are more important for me than that
sadness!
I don't cry,
Only because my friends always do something unique for me
to make me happy!
Friends too are my family.
I don't cry,
Only because my sister is there with me always!
I don't cry,
Because my family always says, In front of any situation stay
strong to face that problem!
I don't cry,
Because I am blessed.
I don't cry,
Because my parents can predict by my face that how much
pain i have and they do something amazing for me through
which my sadness goes that fast like a deer!
I don't cry,
Only and only because my parents love me too much and
cares for me!

Abhigna Mudigonda
<u>An Ode to Ethical Values !!!</u>

Oh, ethical values !
We the people are dreamers,
addicted to play the role of streamers.
in the midst of life's game,
scouting for someone to blame.

Oh, ethical values !
between all those hurdles of endurance,
Bolstering our mind and soul is a hindrance.
Therefore, we entrenched you,
in the vitality of fate's avenue.

Oh, ethical values !
We expected to discard the shabby essence,
and to set up the parity flourescence.
But you confused us,
Because you aren't the same for all of us.

Yet, this is an Ode to you,
as we can't whisper a fond adieu.
Since we know it isn't you who has to change,
but we, the drabby humans have to change

pg. 99

Deepesh Pathak
An ode to teacher

The very first day I thought
You acted like pedagogue
But deep inside I knew
I myself was badly rogue

Beyond all the scientific theories
Formulas, proofs and divergence
You taught me how in this life
To live with zeal and confidence

I still smile today with affection
When I remember the day I got slap
But today I owe you my success
Because it turned out to be claps

You took me towards the right path
From the tunnel of dark iniquity
And acted like a mentor in my life
As my life became serendipity

Ipsita Panigrahi
Live your life...!!!

In search of that light,
which has been going back to rate.
Don't waste your life,
By making it underrate.
Just move on babe.
Your future must be in your wait.
Don't make your life a debate,
Just go straight and ,
Have belief on your fate.
Don't make it a story of hate,
Dear, you will get your ,
Wished desires on your plate .
And for sure, your day will come.
When you will shine like the sun.
You have the potential to create history,
With your victory.
So just do it , before it's too late .
And you will enjoy ,
The flashes of anticipatory

Khushi Kothale
बलिदान!

मैने देखा है मेरे पापा को मौत के मूँह मे झुलते हुए,
क्यूकी मैने देखा है मेरे पापा को सरहद की हिफ़ज़त करते हुए!

मैने देखा है मेरे पापा को बाहादुरी दिखाते हुए,
क्यूकी मैने देखा है मेरे पापा को जंग पे जाते हुए!

मैने देखा है मेरे पापा को बलिदान, त्याग और कुर्बानिया देते हुए,
क्यूकी मैने देखा है मेरे पापा को परिवार छोड के जाते हुए!

मैने देखा है मेरे पापा को रोते हुए,
क्यूकी मैने देखा है उनके दोस्तो को शहीद होते हुए!

मैने देखा है मेरे पापा को हँसते हुए,
क्यूकी मैने देखा है मेरे पापा को घायल होते हुए!

मैने देखा है मेरे पापा को गर्व मेहसूस करते हुए,
क्यूकी मैने देखा है मेरे पापा को Indian Army मे जाते हुए!
क्यूकी मैने देखा है मेरे पापा को सरहद की हिफ़ज़त करते हुए!

Nobil Initha J

In a dipped dark
There was a spark
To draw a pattern of
my goals
To win over
my flaws
To hover over
my success
To arch
my journey of life!

Sameeksha Pimple
<u>Nostalgic dream</u>

A misty illusion was spread over my eyes,
The vision appeared to be the maze of skies.
A short tale of whimsical star verse,
Bring the phase of nostalgic universe.
The meteorite star gazing are the strings of heart,
Wondering it in my cart of art.
An unicorn passed and came backstairs,
Looked at me with quixotic stare.
The curves of cloud and the nerves of crowd
Were musing the fable of rain;
Building of illusions and magical floss
Were the stardust of beauty they gain.
Rhythm and rhyme were in each other's tale;
In the oceanic waves, like a whale!
A beautiful scene was already built,
And my dream was awake and still.

Meghna Chatterjee

An ode to my old days,
I remember those jubilant grins,
In the weltering monsoons,scorching summers and again in
the brightest of springs.
I remember those sweet scribbles on our cute first crushes.
In our mischivous giggles and heartiest laughters we
whiled away those haunting maths classes
Our smiles jubilant, our spirits spontaneous and bright,
I miss those funny squabbles and those hugs warm and
tight.
I miss getting drenched together in the pittar patter rains.
I miss sharing those lunch boxes ,those stupid gossips and
those naive little strokes of pains.
Walking down the memory lane my eyes smile again those
joyful tears.
I miss those carefree teenage days ,I miss those golden
years.

Flairs and Glairs, a platform by a student for the students. We are esteemed youth struggling to carve out our path for our future and we follow a basic mindset Since everyone is not born with all-round skills. Joining hands with people who are born to execute it with perfection is the best way to evolve. Self-Evolution is the need of the hour but, evolving as a community is what we strive for. The initiative as kickstarted by, Founder- Mr. Shubham Shah with the motive to utilize the skillset and talent of writing has now a team of 10+ people who are actively participating into newer forms of learning and discovering talents among youngsters. We Provide platform and services like Publishing opportunities, Open mics, Workshops, Hands-on training. Operating with Brand Name Of Flairs and Glairs (Publication House), we offer the chance of elevating a passionate writer to an esteemed author With Brand name Teekhe Zasbaaat, We bring to you an opportunity to get accustomed with the Public Speaking and Presenting of Thoughts along with regular challenges to brush up your inking spirit. The newest initiative to extend our services we introduced in a new writing Platform- The Glittering Fables and Ink Over Tears.

We Choose to Fly Like A Falcon than to be a

Leg Pulling Crab.

To Know More: Infoline – 7781900870
Mail Us At-
flairsandglairs@gmail.com / info@flairsandglairs.in
Or Visit is at
www.flairsandglairs.com / www.flairsandglairs.in
Social Handles- @flairsandglairs @teekhezasbaaat